ANIMALS ON THE FARM

Pigs

by Christina Leighton

BELLWETHER MEDIA · MINNEAPOLIS, MN

Note to Librarians, Teachers, and Parents:

Blastoff! Readers are carefully developed by literacy experts and combine standards-based content with developmentally appropriate text.

Level 1 provides the most support through repetition of high-frequency words, light text, predictable sentence patterns, and strong visual support.

Level 2 offers early readers a bit more challenge through varied simple sentences, increased text load, and less repetition of high-frequency words.

Level 3 advances early-fluent readers toward fluency through increased text and concept load, less reliance on visuals, longer sentences, and more literary language.

Level 4 builds reading stamina by providing more text per page, increased use of punctuation, greater variation in sentence patterns, and increasingly challenging vocabulary.

Level 5 encourages children to move from "learning to read" to "reading to learn" by providing even more text, varied writing styles, and less familiar topics.

Whichever book is right for your reader, Blastoff! Readers are the perfect books to build confidence and encourage a love of reading that will last a lifetime!

This edition first published in 2018 by Bellwether Media, Inc.

No part of this publication may be reproduced in whole or in part without written permission of the publisher. For information regarding permission, write to Bellwether Media, Inc., Attention: Permissions Department, 5357 Penn Avenue South, Minneapolis, MN 55419.

Library of Congress Cataloging-in-Publication Data

Names: Leighton, Christina, author.
Title: Pigs / by Christina Leighton.
Description: Minneapolis, MN : Bellwether Media, Inc., [2018] | Series:
    Blastoff! Readers. Animals on the Farm | Includes bibliographical
    references and index. | Audience: Age 5-8. | Audience: K to Grade 3.
Identifiers: LCCN 2017029538 | ISBN 9781626177253 (hardcover : alk. paper) |
    ISBN 9781681035055 (ebook)
Subjects: LCSH: Swine–Juvenile literature. | CYAC: Pigs.
Classification: LCC SF395.5 .L45 2018 | DDC 636.4–dc23
LC record available at https://lccn.loc.gov/2017029538

Editor: Rebecca Sabelko   Designer: Lois Stanfield

Printed in the United States of America, North Mankato, MN.

Table of Contents

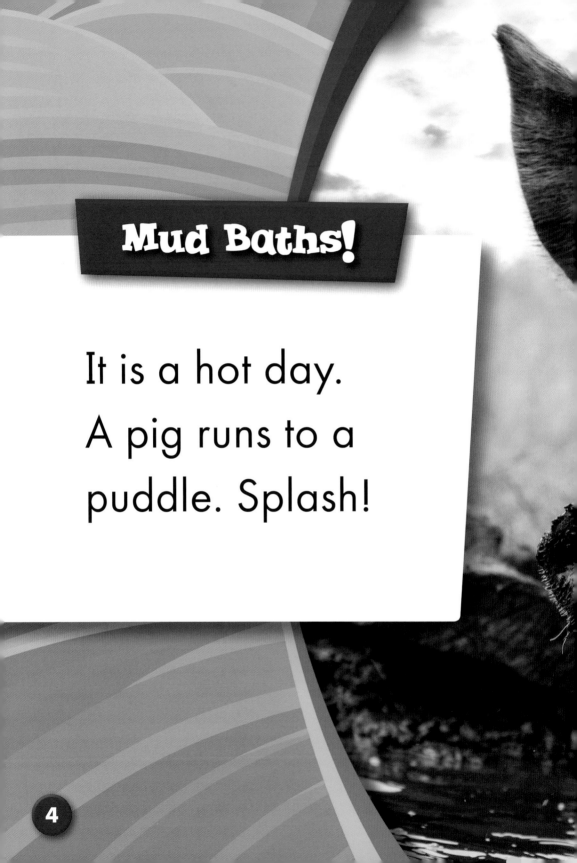

Mud Baths!

It is a hot day. A pig runs to a puddle. Splash!

The pig **wallows** in the mud to keep cool.

What Are Pigs?

Pigs are **mammals**. They have thick, round bodies.

NAMES:

males:	boars
females:	sows
babies:	piglets

9

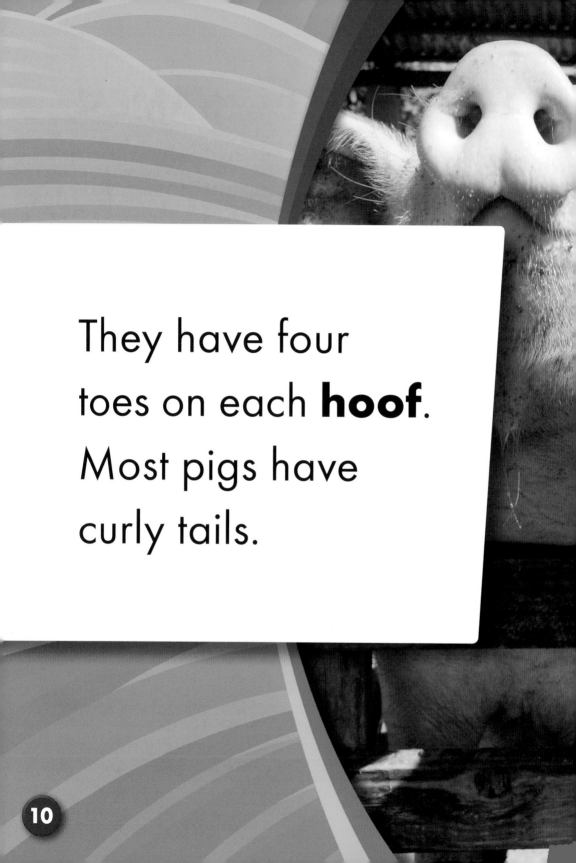

They have four toes on each **hoof**. Most pigs have curly tails.

hoof

11

Many pigs are pink. But they can be different colors, too.

piglets

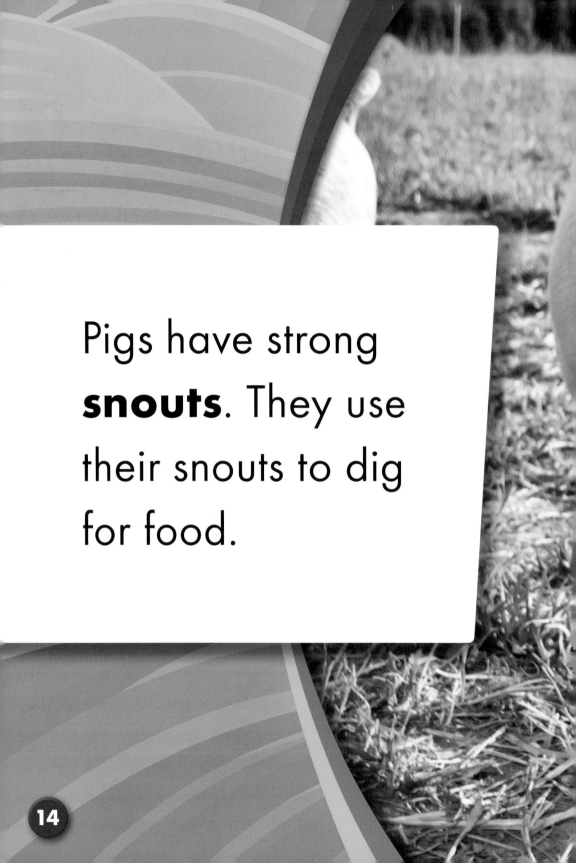

Pigs have strong **snouts**. They use their snouts to dig for food.

snout

Pigs rest in barns or pens. Sometimes, outdoor pigpens have puddles to roll in!

Pigs often eat **roots** and **insects**. They also get food from farmers.

FAVORITE FOODS:
roots, insects, feed

The pigs drink and eat a lot. Here comes the farmer with food. Dinnertime!

Glossary

hoof

a hard covering on the foot of a pig

roots

the underground parts of plants and trees that take in water

insects

small animals with six legs and three separate body sections

snouts

the noses of pigs

mammals

warm-blooded animals that have hair and feed their young milk

wallows

rolls and lies in mud

To Learn More

AT THE LIBRARY
Kuskowski, Alex. *Piglets*. Minneapolis, Minn.:
ABDO Publishing Company, 2014.

Leaf, Christina. *Baby Pigs*. Minneapolis, Minn.:
Bellwether Media, 2014.

Stiefel, Chana. *Pigs on the Family Farm*.
Berkeley Heights, N.J.: Enslow Publishers,
2013.

ON THE WEB
Learning more about pigs
is as easy as 1, 2, 3.

1. Go to www.factsurfer.com.

2. Enter "pigs" into the search box.

3. Click the "Surf" button and you will see a
   list of related web sites.

With factsurfer.com, finding more information
is just a click away.

Index

The images in this book are reproduced through the courtesy of: Eric Isselee, front cover; aleksander hunta, pp. 4-5; Rachael Burke, pp. 6-7; kvasilev, pp. 8-9; RD-SunPhotography, pp. 10-11; Fabiano's_Photo, pp. 12-13; talseN, pp. 14-15; Ewais, pp. 16-17; Erika J Mitchell, pp. 18-19; anandoart, pp. 20-21; CAPTAIN_HOOK, p. 22 (top left); Meister Photos, p. 22 (middle left); ludovikus, p. 22 (bottom left); mike_expert, p. 22 (top right); Perfect Lazybones, p. 22 (middle right); aaltair, p. 22 (bottom right).